Table of Contents

Getting Started .2
What Are Fossils? 4
How Do Fossils Form? 7
Who Studies Fossils? 10
How Are Fossils Collected? 13
Index 16

by Eric Michaels

Getting Started

Millions of years ago, life on Earth was very different from the way it is today. The plants and animals then did not look like those you see today.

The land was different, too. Long ago, there might have been lakes where there are mountains now. The places that are cool and dry now might have been green, warm tropical forests long ago.

How do we know what Earth was like millions of years ago? **Fossils** give us many clues. Let's dig deep and learn about fossils!

What Are Fossils?

There are many kinds of fossils. Some people think of dinosaur bones when they think of fossils. But fossils are like a picture, or print, of things that lived on Earth long ago. A fossil can show all or part of a plant or an animal. It can even show a footprint that was made by a living thing from long ago.

Fossils have shown up in some odd places! Many insect fossils have been found in pieces of **amber**. Amber is tree sap that has hardened. The insects got stuck in the sap. Later, when the sap hardened, it trapped the insect forever.

Huge animals called **mammoths** used to live on Earth. Long ago, some mammoths were trapped in ice. These bodies trapped in ice are a kind of fossil, too.

How Do Fossils Form?

Most fossils are formed from the sand or mud that sits at the bottom of water. When animals and plants die in or near the water, they are covered with this muddy soil, called **sediment**. After a very long time, the sediment turns into rock, and a fossil is formed.

Very hard things like bones and shells slowly **decay**, or rot, in sediment. Sometimes they leave behind a space that is filled in with other material. This material hardens. This makes a **cast** of the bone or shell that used to be there.

When some plants and animals decay, something called **carbon** is left behind. The black carbon shows the shape of the once-living things. These carbon outlines are also fossils.

Other fossils are formed when minerals from water soak into dead plants or animals. These dead things do not decay, because the minerals make them hard like stone.

Who Studies Fossils?

Did you know that some people hunt for fossils as a part of their job? **Paleontologists** (pay-lee-uhn-TAH-luh-jists) are scientists who study the remains of plants and animals that lived long, long ago. These scientists collect and study fossils and sort them for museums.

What do paleontologists learn when they study fossils? Fossils help them learn how plants, animals, and Earth have changed over time.

Paleontologists can tell how old rocks are by looking at fossils in the rocks. Rocks with fossils of shells or sea animals can tell scientists that the land where the fossils were found may have once been an ocean.

Oil is often found in rocks that have fossils in them. So the study of rocks and fossils is also helpful to oil companies. It can help them know where to drill underground for oil.

How Are Fossils Collected?

When paleontologists find a fossil, they use special tools to remove it. A small shovel might be used to remove a fossil from soft ground. But if a fossil is in rock, the job is more difficult. It might have to be removed with a hammer and chisel.

Inside a lab, paleontologists use smaller tools to chip away any rock that is still around the fossil. If a fossil is in pieces, the scientists put it back together like a puzzle.

Fossils of animal bones can sometimes be put together to form a skeleton. A strong frame is used to hold the bones together. A museum might show the skeleton.

You can search for fossils, too! The next time you're outside, try to find one. Then try to tell if it's from a plant or an animal. Just think, you could be holding something that is millions of years old!

Index

amber, 5

animal(s), 2, 4, 6–11, 14, 15

bone(s), 4, 7, 14

carbon, 8

cast, 7

dinosaur, 4

footprint, 4

insect(s), 5

mammoths, 6

minerals, 9

oil, 12

paleontologists, 10, 11, 13

plant(s), 2, 4, 7–10, 15

print, 4

rock(s), 7, 11–13

sap, 5

sediment, 7

shell(s), 7, 11

skeleton, 14

tools, 13